PUFFIN BOOKS

WHAT A COMIC RELIEF!

Dear Reader

What a bit of luck! When we were asked to write this Comic Relief book, we thought it was a good chance to suck up to parents, who often think comedians are stupid, and so we wrote a really sensible book on subjects like Table Manners, Medieval History and What To Do If The Entire Royal Family Comes To Tea.

Fortunately, however, Puffin asked a couple of young editors to look at it, named William and Jemima Brat, and they've turned our very serious and educational work into a disgraceful collection of misspellings and misconduct. We couldn't be more delighted – so all that's left to us to say is a Big, Big Thank You for buying the book. Money from it goes to Comic Relief, and you've really made a difference to someone's life by buying it.

This year, two thirds of the money raised by Comic Relief goes to help people in Sudan and Ethiopia and other African countries, including Mozambique where war is making life impossible for ordinary people, and Burkina Faso, where we hope to help an extraordinary project that turns desert into farmland.

We're spending the other third of the money in Britain to help young people who are homeless, or who have physical disabilities or problems with drugs or alcohol. And we are now going to give money to the elderly too – people like your grandparents and ours whose lives are often hard and very lonely.

We hope you enjoy the book a lot, and if your parents don't like bits of it, say that you only bought it to help Comic Relief, and that, in fact, you've got no intention of reading it – you only need it for propping up your wobbly desk at school.

Best of luck to you and lots of thanks from

Everyone at Comic Relief
Red Nose Headquarters of the World

RED
NOSE

WHAT A COMIC RELIEF!

The Incredibly Naughty Survive At School Handbook

Cunningly compiled by Huw Tristan Davies,
with brilliant contributions from Alan Rowe, Patrick Gallagher,
Mark Rodgers, Ed McHenry, Michael Peek, Tony Husband
and Kev F Sutherland

Puffin Books

PUFFIN BOOKS
Published by the Penguin Group
27 Wrights Lane, London W8 5TZ, England
Viking Penguin Inc., 40 West 23rd Street, New York, New York 10010, USA
Penguin Books Australia Ltd, Ringwood, Victoria, Australia
Penguin Books Canada Ltd, 2801 John Street, Markham, Ontario, Canada L3R 1B4
Penguin Books (NZ) Ltd, 182-190 Wairau Road, Auckland 10, New Zealand

Penguin Books Ltd, Registered Offices: Harmondsworth, Middlesex, England

First published 1989
10 9 8 7 6 5 4 3 2 1

Made and printed in Great Britain by Richard Clay Ltd, Bungay, Suffolk

CONTENTS

FOOT INSPECTION

INTRODUCTION

by William and Jemima Brat, BA, BBC
(Bloomin' Amazing, Brilliantly Brainy Children)

Oi! Stop picking your noses
and pay attention at the back!

This ~~hilary hilarary~~ very funny book
is called <u>The Incredibly Naughty S(urvive)
A(t) S(chool) Handbook.</u> You'll know that
already if you've read the cover. If you
haven't, then why are you reading this bit
first? R U A loony?

The ~~stupid~~ clever old stoats at Puffin
Books (smarm, smarm, suck up, lick, dribble)
wanted an ~~authordentist or theantique~~ real
book about how to survive in school today.

Because they went to school with Henry
VIII, and because we are utterly brill,
hard-working and like Wet Wet Wet, they
asked us to do it. They also asked us
because Jemima Threatened to put dead
cockroaches and ants down their pants if
they didn't.

The main ~~purple-porpoise~~ aim of the book
is ~~to help you get into very very serious
trouble~~ to help you get the most out of being in school.
The other aim is to ~~tease~~ help people a lot.

All the profits go to Comic Relief
charities (not us, worse luck), so when
you buy it you can have a giant giggle AND
learn something AND do something useful-all
at the same time. Which is more than you can
say for school.

Get ~~stuffed~~ reading,
lots of love,
William and Jemima

William + Jemima

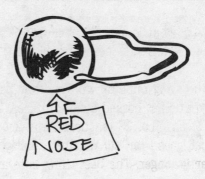

RED
NOSE

1 NOT GOING TO SCHOOL

FIRST of all, what is school? Some say it's a big building where kids go to learn lessons. Well 'SNOT.

School is a big building where clever people (i.e. Brats like us)go and get bossed around by real old thickies who look like stoats (i.e. PE teachers) and are held prisoner 'till the bell goes – or 'till we finish our greens – whichever is longer. The best thing is to avoid it completely.

There is only one way of getting out of going to school for ever and ever, and that's to grow up. IT CAN TAKE

AGES. If you are really cunning and follow our advice in this chapter, you'll find out how to get out of the really bad days.

REMEMBER: It's impossible to go to school if you are stuck at home. There are three ways to make sure you ARE stuck at home.
1) Hold yourself hostage in your own room until tea-time.
2) Write your own sick note.
3) Pretend to have lost your memory.

1) Holding yourself hostage in your own bedroom until tea-time

(You'll need a bedroom, lemon and lime jelly cubes and two very stupid parents – easy if Mum and Dad are PE teachers.)
THE PLAN:
a) Pour melted green jelly on to stairs and floor outside your bedroom. Smear door handle so parents can't open it.
b) Leave a note telling them little green men and women from Mars arrived in the night and are holding you and three of your sister's Sindy dolls hostage.
c) Write this ransom note: Dear Parents, Leave a quarterpounder with cheese, two regular fries and a large Coke outside the door RIGHT NOW and we'll release the dolls. Mess with us and we'll eat your son/daughter! Signed, Little green men and women from Mars.
d) Hope your parents can read (if they're PE teachers they probably can't). Eat quarterpounder and wipe hands on bedspread – it's ok if no one's watching.
e) Wait till tea-time and release yourself, smearing more green jelly over the window panes for good effect.

PS: Only do this in term time. Being stuck in your bedroom all day in the holidays is ALMOST as boring as going to school – especially if you are covered in jelly.

2) How to write your own sick note

A SICK note is another brill way to bunk off school – and
the sicker it is the better. Luckily our Mum and Dad –
Mr and Mrs Brat – have forgotten how to write, so we've
scribbled our own. Just this once we'll let you copy:

Dear teacher,
unfortunately Jemima/William is ill today.
Of course she/he tried to go to school but
when she/he woke up all green and frothing
at the mouth and with both ears having
dropped off in the night, I said, COR blimey
charlie NO! Without any ears she/he wouldn't
have been able to hear anything and would
learn even less than normal.
 The docter came, and as soon as he saw
William/Jemima, he also frothed at the mouth,
rolled over, lay on his back and said 'I am a
stoat' we called a second docter, who was
sad to say the first docter was now mad
but was more positive about William/
Jemima. He said the ears might grow back
after a days rest in front of the telly.
 The docter added that by tomorrow
William/Jemima might be cured and amazingly,
show no signs of having been absolutely the
sickest person in the history of the world. This
has nothing to do with the fact that tomorrow
is saturday.
            yours insincerely,
                Mrs Brat
PS If my handwriting looks exactly like
williams/Jemimas that's because I'm so
worried about his/her health I've clean
forgotten how to write.

12

3) How to pretend to have lost your memory

OF COURSE if you're really desperate not to go to school, try our special memory trick – if you can remember it!

Come downstairs and talk to your mother like this:

MUM: Morning, darling.
YOU: Who on earth are you?
MUM: I beg your pardon?
YOU: I should think so too. Where's my mother?
MUM: But I am your mother, William.
YOU: What did you call me?
MUM: William.
YOU: My name's *William*?
MUM: Yes. Now stop being silly and sit down and eat your breakfast.
YOU: My what?

Carry on until the doctor arrives and recommends you spend the day resting at home surrounded by familiar objects and eating lots of familiar sweeties.

Getting caught out of school can lead to immediate expulsion...

... unless, of course, you give teacher a note.

William: What's the easiest way to get out of school, Jemima?
Jemima: Through the gate, stupid.

WELL READ NOSE

WORK AND LESSONS

One of the smelliest things about school – apart from the drains, PE and macaroni cheese, must be all the work and lessons you have to do.

The two things, though, which are absolutely the worst are science and writing essays about what we did on our holidays. We got so fed up copying out the same old rubbish, we invented some new rubbish!

William and Jemima Brat's Instant What-we-did-on-our-holidays Essay

Simply copy out this essay filling in the gaps with a word of your choice from the appropriate list. The result

p.t.o. →

will be brilliant and win you top marks – or 500 lines if someone else has bought the book and has the same bright idea.

This ..[a].. I went to..[b].. with my ..[c]...

We stayed in ..[d].. and I slept in a ..[e].. which I

had to ..[f].. with my ..[g]...

The weather was very ..[h].. and Dad complained

about the ..[i].., which he said was too ..[j]...

We had a lot of ..[k].. when we played at

the ..[l].. and we pushed ..[m].. into the ..[n]...

It was a wonderful ..[o].. and the best ..[p]..

I have ever ..[q]... I hope we go back there ..[r]...

[a]	[b]	[c]
summer	Blackpool	family
Xmas	Transylvania	suitcase
Easter	The Amazon jungle	pet fish
Hallowe'en	the Post Office	killer zombie

[d]
a boarding house
a shed
Dracula's Castle
a slime pit

[e]
camp bed
bucket
bath of acid
dung heap

[f]
share
eat
empty
clean

[g]
cousin
killer zombie
octopus
teeth

[h]
hot
cold
windy
wet

[i]
food
beach
room
car park
bucket

[j]
small
runny
far from the toilet
radioactive
full of jelly

[k]
fun
trouble
laughs
injuries
boils

[l]
swimming pool
roadworks
zoo
funfair
sewer outlet

[m]
Dad
Mum
whelks
passers-by

[n]
water
tiger's cage
dodgems
path-of-a-
  steamroller

[o]
experience
holiday
Xmas
bucket

[p]
laugh
fun
jelly
goat

[q]
had
eaten
juggled
disintegrated

[r]
soon
never
next year
when I get out
  of hospital

18

SCIENCE is dull, dull, dull except when we do live experiments in the lab. Our fave is to put worms down the back of the School Swot's trousers and time how long it takes him to scream like a big sissy. There are loads of other ways to make a nuisance of yourself:

Experiments you CAN do in the school laboratory without getting really bored
Using a clean test tube, an old lavatory roll and some fluffy bits from a stoat's belly-button, do the following experiments:

★ Cross a PE teacher with an elephant to produce an elephant in a tracksuit who can't do joined-up writing.

★ Set fire to the School Cook's chair – preferably with the School Cook sitting in it – to produce a sat-alight dish.

★ Cross the School Bully with a mad squirrel and produce a complete and utter nutter.

★ Cross the School Chaplain with a chimney and throw in bits of killer spider to produce a praying mantelpiece.

★ Try crossing the Cricket Coach with a lump of wood to come up with something completely batty.

SCIENCE LESSON: TESTING THE THEORY OF GRAVITY

Experiments you CANNOT do in the school science laboratory

For thousands of years scientists have tried to re-create the yellow gunge School Cook puts in our macaroni cheese. THIS IS EXTREMELY DANGEROUS AND MUST NOT UNDER ANY CIRCUMSTANCES BE ATTEMPTED BY UNQUALIFIED STUDENTS.

For what to do if School Cook tries to serve macaroni cheese – and how to evacuate a school in under ten minutes – see the chapter on School Dinners – BUT ONLY IF YOU HAVE A VERY STRONG STOMACH.

OF COURSE all lessons are naff and boring unless you play the really BAD game William and I invented. It's the only thing known to Man and Woman to get you through double history:

The Brat Anti-Boredom Technique
With your snotty little friends, think up a completely ridiculous word before Teach arrives. The idea is to make Teach say the chosen word before the end of the lesson.

For example, if it's history you might choose 'washing machine' and the lesson might go like this:

> TEACHER: After conquering Western Europe, Napoleon and his army set out east to conquer Russia...
> YOU: Please, Miss? How did they keep their clothes clean on the march?
> TEACHER: They didn't.
> YOUR FRIEND: You mean they wore dirty clothes?
> TEACHER: That's right.
> ANOTHER FRIEND: Couldn't they have taken something along with them to clean the clothes with?
> TEACHER: I suppose they could (IRRITATED). They probably had soap.

YET ANOTHER FRIEND: So they did them by hand?
TEACHER: Yes, I suppose so. Anyway
(ANNOYED), as I was saying, they marched from
Paris...
YOU: Couldn't they have done them with something
electrical?
TEACHER: Oh, do stop talking nonsense Brat – I
mean, you don't honestly think they carried
washing machines with them, do you?!!!???

DING DING DING!!!!

You win – start the next lesson with a new word.

EXTREMELY IMPORTANT PS: Lessons, unlike most
other things in life, have a definite beginning, middle and
end. That means that if you can stay awake, you can
plot your EXACT position in a lesson.

HOW TO DO IT: From the point you are in a lesson,
draw a line vertically down until you run off the edge of
the lesson. The lesson is now divided into two parts.

Give the first to a friend and then run away. Take the
second part, cover it in chopped tomatoes, onions,
oregano and peppers, and stand back in amazement. You
have created a pizza! What's that if it's not learning
something?

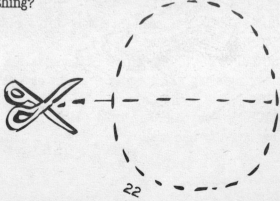

WOODWORK LESSONS

5 WAYS TO PUT A FREE PERIOD TO GOOD USE

1) Call a meeting of the Escape Committee, and continue digging your tunnel.

2) Block up the staff-room door with a large object (e.g. school piano, elephant, Russell Grant), so that your next period will also be teacher-free.

3) Paint spots on your face, so teacher will send you home. (Don't do this if you've got one of those spotty young teachers, or he'll think you're making fun of him.)

4) Smear your exercise books with chicken giblets and tempt a stray dog to savage them, so you've an excuse for not handing your homework in.

5) Do the 1,000,000 lines you've been given for trying the preceding 4 ruses in your last free period.

History teacher: Tell the class, William, what it would have been like to be a schoolboy at the time of William the Conqueror.
William: Well, for a start there would have been nearly 1000 years less history to learn.

Jemima: What do you do when cracks start to appear on the classroom blackboard during break?
William: Read them quickly before teacher rubs them out.

Knock knock.
Who's there?
Lesson.
Lesson who?
Lesson very carefully because I won't say it again.

History teacher: Where was Charles I's death-warrant signed?
Jemima: At the bottom, of course.

Never feel embarrassed about offering teacher an apple before lessons...

...the delight shown on her face will make it all worthwhile.

CHAPTER 3

SCHOOL DINNERS

W. and J. BRAT OFFICIAL HEALTH WARNING: Reading this chapter – and eating school dinners like spotted duck-billed platypus and Lancashire hot pit bull terrier – can make your tummy grumble.

What to do if they serve macaroni cheese

★ DO NOT TOUCH IT – school macaroni cheese (SMC) is one of the most dangerous substances known to man and woman.

★ Evacuate the dining hall quickly and calmly.

★ Take all school pets with you – it's not fair to leave them in the building alone with Cook – and assemble in the playground.

★ If the SMC is hot and steaming, seal off your town and move to Milton Keynes. If you live in Milton Keynes already, tough.

★ When SMC develops a thick spotty skin – it will if it's *real* SMC – pour hundreds of gallons of liquid concrete into the dining hall.

★ Bulldoze your school. Bury the building under 10,000 tons of sand and a 10ft layer of lead-and-steel-reinforced granite. Go on holiday for a very long time.

How to become the School Cook

Cooking is an art and quali-whatnot-ifications are vital if you want to be a chef. Don't believe it! We have found a secret copy of the Government's *Training Manual for Cooks* and just look at the page we have printed below.

CHEF AT THE RITZ:
Cordon Bleu excelsior course
Three years as trainee cook
Four years as an under-cook
Degree in sauce-making
Diploma in desserts

COOK AT BERNI INN:
One year catering course

COOK AT MACDONALD'S:
One week catering course

SCHOOL COOK AT St BRATS' SCHOOL:
Two arms and at least eight fingers

So, if you're eating sausages at St Brats, keep your eyes peeled for those other two fingers!!!

29

THE SCHOOL KITCHEN

PACKED LUNCH

Where to put school food

YOU don't have to eat school food. In fact, we don't recommend you do. Here are five alternative places to put your food – we've given them star ratings:

1) INTO YOUR MOUTH
STAR RATING: 0
COMMENT: Really dumb. This'll make you sick for rest of the day.

2) ON TO THE PLATE OF THE PERSON SITTING NEXT TO YOU:
STAR RATING: ★★
COMMENT: Not bad if the person is a wimp. Not good if they're bigger than you and put it straight back on your plate with a bit of extra cabbage.

3) INTO YOUR POCKET
STAR RATING: ★
COMMENT: If the grub looks bad on your plate, think
how grotty it'll feel dripping down your leg in 20 minutes'
time.

4) INTO YOUR SPECIALLY PREPARED POCKET
STAR RATING: ★★
COMMENT: Line your pocket with a plastic bag, and
when no one is watching, slip the muck into it. Throw
the bag away after the meal, but make sure your bag
doesn't have holes in it.

5) ON TO THE PLATE OF YOUR PE TEACHER
STAR RATING: ★★★★★★★★★★★★★★★★★★★★
COMMENT: Easily the best plan. Firstly, PE teachers are
usually too busy doing press-ups to notice what you put
on their plates, and secondly they are said to be the only
living species that needs to eat cabbage that has been
boiled for five days solid to survive.

DEAD NOSE

While the Majority of school food appears dull and boring...

... the good that it does for you cannot be over-stressed.

RED TOJE

CHAPTER 4

GAMES

TO BE good at games you have to enjoy standing half naked in an icy gale and be spattered with cold lumps of mud while the PE teacher (wearing TWO nylon tracksuits) blows his or her whistle to keep warm.

The only creature that's happy running around in shorts in the freezing cold in long wet grass is the stoat – not William or Jemima Brat, thank you very much.

How to get out of doing sport altogether
★ Wrap yourself in brown paper, stick a £1.80 stamp on your head and post yourself to Majorca.

★ Sew up all the school's basketball and netball nets, cut down the goal posts and drain the swimming pool. (To make extra sure you get out of swimming, paint extremely large, drippy verrucas on to the soles of your feet.)

★ Donate at least three of your internal body organs to medical research.

If you're REALLY unlucky you can donate all your internal organs to medical science and STILL be picked for the school hockey or rugby team. Make sure you're extra specially cruddy so you never get picked again:

How to be dropped from any sports team you can think of

★ Never run during games – it's tiring and causes accidents.

★ If it's unavoidable – that is, if you're being chased by the PE teacher's pet sabre-toothed tiger – ALWAYS run in the opposite direction to the ball.

★ If a team-mate accidentally gives you the ball, GIVE IT STRAIGHT BACK – PREFERABLY TO THE OTHER SIDE.

★ If you ever find a ball at your feet, dribble furiously – FROM THE MOUTH.

★ Wear ALL the right equipment: for judo, rounders and five-aside football you need flippers, a snorkel and lots and lots of bandages.

★ Remember, it is not winning that's important. It is how many points you can score for the OTHER SIDE (before your games teacher suspects) that counts.

P.E. LESSONS CAN BE FUN

ONLY two words really matter in sport. But having the skill – and timing – to use them properly is rare.

When to say 'PASS' and when to say 'PANCREAS'

'Pass' is the most important word in team games and you should yell it out keenly whenever you see the teacher looking at you.

If someone does pass you the ball, speed of reaction is then vital. You must fall to your knees before the ball reaches you, and shout: 'Oh dear, oh dear, I think I've ruptured my pancreas.'

Even if the teacher doesn't believe you, you'll still score some points for knowing the word 'pancreas'.

If you're still hellbent on wearing baggy shorts that scratch your thighs while running up and down in the freezing cold and having the PE teacher blow a whistle at you, try these Brat-approved alternative sports:

Alternative school sports

★ VOLLEY BALL: Volley balls – or to give them their correct spelling, *Vol-et-Bals* – are bite-sized morsels of puff pastry with a creamy, eggy filling that are thrown over a net.

The aim is to catch them in your mouth before they bounce, and eat them. The first team to make itself sick is the winner.

★ HOCKEY: This is not a sport but Spanish for 'OK'.

★ RUGBY: A town in east Warwickshire. Do not play it.

It has a population of thousands and unless you have a very big team you will lose.

★ CROSS-COUNTRY RUNNING: This is for young people who like running but who get cross about Britain's countryside being spoilt. The further they run, the crosser they become.

★ CROSS-CHANNEL SWIMMING: Only people who know how to swim should try this. If you can only do two lengths of the baths with your Mr T arm bands, take the ferry.

SWIMMING LESSONS

Try and show as much enthusiasm as you can on the sportsfield...

... with that attitude you are certain to go far.

William: What's the quickest way to get out of PE?
Jemima: Jump on a High Speed Train-ing Shoe.

RED ROSE

SCHOOL TRIPS

School trips are a great way to escape lessons so long as the coach driver doesn't remember you from last year and ban you from the bus.

Unfortunately, you must pay attention as you'll probably have to write an essay about it later. Here are some clues to help you work out where those wicked teachers have taken you.

There are lots of old bones all over the place and animals hanging up that don't look like stoats

Tricky. You may be in the school kitchens, but it's more likely you're on a visit to the National Museum of Dead Animals and Old Bits of Bone that Grown-Ups Pretend Are Very Interesting.

This is an extremely boring place and you are usually only taken there as punishment or if it's raining. Its proper name is the Natural History Museum. THIS IS RIDICULOUS. There's nothing natural about keeping dead animals inside a building.

You are surrounded by dummies, some of whom you recognize

You are either in the school staff room or you are visiting the local waxworks. There's one way to find out if the person in front of you is a brainless nerd or just a harmless waxwork model: put a live stoat up his or her jumper.

If there's no reaction and the person appears completely dead, you're talking to your history teacher.

Everybody is speaking French

Either you are at home watching 'Allo 'Allo, or you are on a day-trip to Calais and are stuck in fog at Dover.

You are in a damp, smelly cave furnished with old cardboard boxes as tables and car tyres as chairs

Your class has been so well behaved that you are all invited for tea at the headmaster's new luxury bungalow. (Don't worry, this is only a bad dream.)

A DAY TRIP TO THE ZOO

43

It is essential that you make the most out of any trips to the zoo...

... it is amazing what can be learnt there.

How to organize your own school trip

Stand outside your school with a long length of rope or string. Ask a friend to hold the other end and stretch it across the path of the school. When the school takes more than three steps forward it will trip!

ONCE YOU have wrecked the coach, it can sometimes be hard to know what to do on a long journey. Fear not! Help is at hand! Try these fiendishly clever quizzes on your next school trip and find out who really is the thickest student in the school.

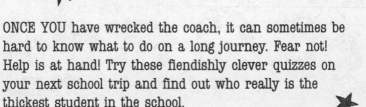

IT'S TIME FOR OUR BRAIN TEASING, TIME WASTING...

QUIZ and PICTURE PUZZLE ★ PARADE

ODD ONE OUT

CAN YOU FIND THE ODD ONE OUT IN THE 2 GROUPS HERE?

1
FOOTBALL
HOCKEY
NETBALL
CRICKET
FENCING
TENNIS
RUGBY
BASEBALL

2

KOOKABURRA KANGAROO

KOALA ROLF HARRIS KIWI

The Common Denominator **3**

THESE FOUR CHARACTERS ALL HAVE SOMETHING IN COMMON, WHAT CAN IT BE?

HENRY the VIII BONZO CHIMP

ROBIN HOOD NAPOLEON

4 DO YOU KNOW?

IF YOU HAVE A REFEREE IN FOOTBALL, AND AN UMPIRE IN CRICKET...

WHAT DO YOU GET IN BOWLS?

5 DO YOU KNOW?

IF YOU GET A PRIDE OF LIONS, AND A HERD OF CATTLE...

WHAT DO YOU GET IN PACKS?

What's this? ⑥

IN AFRICA I CHASED TIGERS ON HORSEBACK

What is wrong with this statement? ⑦

⑧ WHAT ARE OPTICS?

FIND THE BIRD ⑨

STUDY THIS PICTURE AND IT WILL SUGGEST THE NAME OF A BIRD, CAN YOU SPOT IT?

⑩ A QUICK AND EASY CROSSWORD

DOWN
1. ELEPHANT
ACROSS
1. 747 PLANE

⑪ # SPOT THE DIFFERENCE!

WHY IS PICTURE A DIFFERENT FROM PICTURE B?

12 DO YOU KNOW?

IF BARN OWLS LIVE IN BARNS...

WHERE DO YOU FIND BATS?

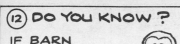

13 COMPLETE THE LIST

Fill in the missing word

YOGI BEAR
FUZZY BEAR
RUPERT BEAR
PADDINGTON _____

14

THIS IS THE LONE RANGER and TONTO, WHO IS SILVER?

15

WHO IN HISTORY WAS HALF MAN-HALF ANIMAL?

16

HERE WE GO
HERE WE GO

Why did Humpty Dumpty think it funny when he fell off the wall?

AT THE ZOO 17

Find the letters that only appear once, then you can make something you might see at the zoo.

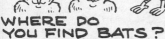

K	T	A	S	H
T	L	T	A	G
H	S	I	K	H
S	K	G	O	T
A	G	H	G	N

JIM'S STRING

18

HOW MANY PIECES OF STRING ARE THERE IN LITTLE JIM'S POCKETS?

47

19 ODD ONE OUT

WHO'S THE ODD ONE OUT IN THE GROUP BELOW?

BOO!

HELLO MUM
THE CREATURE

KING KONG

GODZILLA

THE MONSTER

20 NUTS

HOW MANY NUTS CAN YOU SEE IN THIS PICTURE?

21 WHAT DO PELICANS LIKE TO EAT?

TAKE AWAY MENU

FD McHENRY

22 Who should never, ever wear glasses when he goes to work?

23 What is a Coat of Arms?

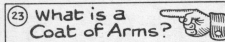

ALL THE ANSWERS
TO READ THE ANSWERS, HOLD THE BOOK UPRIGHT AND STAND ON YOUR HEAD.

1: CRICKET, WHICH IS A SMALL INSECT (THE REST ARE SPORTS.) 2: A KIWI COMES FROM NEW ZEALAND (THE OTHERS ALL COME FROM AUSTRALIA.) 3: NONE OF THEM EVER RODE ON A MOTOR BIKE. 4: GOLDFISH. 5: CARDS 6: A SUGAR CUBE WITH THE MEASLES. 7: TIGERS DON'T RIDE HORSES. 8: FLEAS ON A KANGAROO. 9: NIGHTJAR. 10: 1 DOWN — JUMBO, 1 ACROSS — JUMBO 11: PICTURE 'A' SHOWS 'KING KONG' WHILE PICTURE 'B' SHOWS HIS IDENTICAL TWIN BROTHER, 'HONG KONG', 12: IN CRICKET BAGS. 13: STATION. 14: HE'S THE PIRATE IN 'TREASURE ISLAND,' 15: BUFFALO BILL. 16: BECAUSE IT CRACKED HIM UP. 17: LINO, WHICH YOU WILL SEE ON THE FLOOR OF THE HEAD KEEPERS HUT. 18: NONE, THEY ARE ALL ON DISPLAY IN THE PICTURE. 19: KING KONG (NONE OF THE OTHERS APPEARED IN QUESTION NO.11.) 20: NINE (WHICH INCLUDES THE MAN.) 21: ANYTHING THAT FITS THE BILL. 22: A BOXER. 23: A JACKET FOR AN OCTOPUS.

OTHER PUPILS

One really cruddy thing about school is all the other snotty little creeps who go there. Some are even worse than teachers. Read this chapter and find out how to spot the main types.

How to recognize other pupils

WHO YOUR BEST FRIENDS ARE: They look just like you but have much greasier hair, more spots, bigger verrucas and worse food stains dribbled down the front of their blazers. That's why you like them: by comparison, teachers and parents think YOU look clean.

How to tell if you're teacher's pet

Do you suck up to teachers? Answer this simple quiz to find out just how big a sucker you really are.

1) When a teacher enters the room, what do you say?
a) 'Good morning, O Magnificent One.'
b) 'Look out! Here comes Godzilla!'
c) 'Plug this synthesizer in for me, would you?'
d) 'Have you got any fish?'

2) Which gift would you be most likely to give a teacher?
a) A yummy, scrummy, juicy apple.
b) The address of a good hairdresser.
c) A copy of your latest LP.
d) A bucket of eels.

3) Which of these phrases best describes your exercise books?
a) Neat, clean and full of ticks from teacher.
b) Covered in drawings of Fishface, Ratbag, Baldy, Goggle-eyes and other members of staff.
c) Full of song lyrics about being miserable.
d) Drenched in slime and encrusted with barnacles.

4) Which phrase best describes your view of teachers?
a) Yummy, scrummy, wonderful human beings who should be paid a million pounds a week.
b) Fish-faced, baldy, goggle-eyed ratbags.
c) People with not much money to spend on records. Pretty useless, really.
d) Upright bipedal humanoids who keep you in a tank of water.

HOW DID YOU SCORE?

Mostly As: You are definitely a teacher's pet. You probably did this test without cheating. Creep!

Mostly Bs: You are a teacher's PET HATE. You should try to curb your hostile attitude – unless you hope to become a headmaster.

Mostly Cs: You are not teacher's pet – you are one of the Pet Shop Boys. See a doctor before it's too late.

Mostly Ds: You are a teacher's pet – probably a pet octopus.

TEACHER'S PET

THE D.I.Y. ADOLESCENT KIT

1. SQUIRT OIL ONTO HAIR

2. STICK ON SELF-ADHESIVE SPOTS

3. APPLY BODY ODOUR SPRAY

4. DRAW ON BLACKHEADS WITH BLACKHEAD PENCIL

5. TAKE TWO GRUMPY PILLS

6. FALL IN LOVE

WHOM YOU WOULD MOST LIKE YOUR BEST FRIEND TO BE: This person is in all the school teams, is top in every subject and does not dribble food down the front of his or her blazer. This person is so wonderful he or she *actually does your homework for you.*

Unfortunately, this child does not exist – he or she is a figment of your teacher's and your parents' imagination. ALL CHILDREN DRIBBLE FOOD.

THE SCHOOL SWOT:

★ All swots wear big glasses held on their noses by Elastoplast.

★ Girl swots wear skirts six inches longer than is fashionable and boy swots wear long trousers six inches above the ankle.

★ Swots don't carry briefcases. They have so many books that they have to push them between classes in a wheelbarrow.

★ Swots stay up all night revising for things like morning assembly and how-to-get-on-the-bus.

★ School Rules say that all swots must have very bad dandruff or they may not sit exams. (NB: If a swot shakes his or her head at you, call in the snow ploughs.)

William: How can you tell swots attract insects?
Jemima: Look at their books — they're covered in ticks.

WED NOSES

Always act kindly towards your fellow pupils...

... you never know when you might need them.

Jemima: Why did the thickest boy in the school smack himself over the head?
William: He thought he might be able to knock some sense into himself.

Jemima: Why do you call school dunces 'Gravy' when they catch the mumps?
William: Because they're thick AND lumpy.

CHAPTER

7

TEACHERS AND STAFF

What's the difference between a very old maths teacher and a pet stoat? Easy – the stoat doesn't set homework! There's probably loads of other things you thickos don't know about teachers. For instance, what do they mean when they say 'vile and odious little reptile'? If you don't know, look in the mirror!

This chapter is all about what makes teachers sick ... er ... we mean tick.

Some really horrible facts you didn't know about teachers

★ Many suffer job-related illnesses such as 'blackboard-rubber-thrower's elbow' and 'chalk-licker's finger.'

★ All teachers buy their uniforms at Dull and Dowdy of Ditchwater, which specializes in baggy cord trousers with flies that don't do up properly, nylon shirts with frayed collars, hairy tweed skirts and shapeless mutant cardigans.

★ Teachers never punish anyone without a reason. The most common are that the teacher's car broke down or that the teacher missed last night's episode of *EastEnders*.

Jones Minor my car wouldn't start this morning bend over

★ Half of all teachers must, by law, be overweight. Many skinny ones have to be force-fed beer and cream cakes.

★ Many heads insist that teachers clean blackboards with their tongues.

★ Many teachers sleep on their desks after school and eat the left-over chewing gum that's been stuck under desk lids for them.

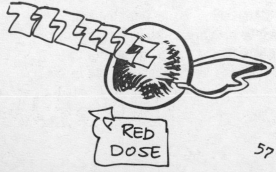

57

THE HEADMASTER

Of course, as we Brats well know, there is one teacher more dangerous and more stupid than all the others put together:

THE PE TEACHER.

He or she can be tall or short, fat or thin, but will always, always wear a whistle and a nylon tracksuit. PE teachers are especially dangerous when they're allowed inside the school to teach other subjects in the periods when they are not running round and round in circles out in the cold.

Five Things You Didn't Know About PE Teachers

1) Most are descended from rugby balls

2) The only thing more stupid than a PE teacher is two PE teachers

3) They never get anywhere in life because they're always running up and down on the spot

4) PE teachers' favourite pathetic joke:
   PE TEACHER: Where's that runner been?
   SCHOOL COOK: In the saucepan with all the others.

Absolutely The Three Worst Teachers of All Time

1) Dr Daniel Druff (known as Dan), biology master at St Itchey's, Scratchwell.

Druff's favourite punishment was to bury pupils up to their necks in the school dandruff pit while making them decline Latin verbs. In 1958 he tripped into the pit while adding some of his own precious white powder. Sadly it was half-term and nobody heard his cries for help.

2) La Contessa di Bendoverissimo, governess of the Ouchalotti School in Tuscany, Italy.

The Contessa was feared for the strict way she forced pupils to eat up every last bit of pizza on their plate – yes, even the dry crusty bit with no tomato sauce on it that's always left over.

In 1632 the nearby Leaning Tower of Pizza fell on the school, sandwiching the Contessa between a Four Seasons and an American Hot with extra pepperoni and cheese to go. She tried to eat her way to safety, but grew incredibly fat and exploded.

Always remove your cap when talking to a teacher...

... your show of respect will not go unnoticed.

3) Dr Algernon Bra (known as Algy) still teaches maths in Milton Keynes, even though he has not spoken properly since 1927 when, after playing squash with Einstein, he decided to communicate using only equations. One day he set his pupils the following problem:

$$i + m + t + t + t + t = ?$$

The answer is simple.

$$i + m + t + t + t + t = im4t$$

im4t = I am forty.

However, they didn't believe him and replied:

$$!! + u + r >>>> 4t < 8t!$$

Which roughly translated means: 'Forty? Pull the other one, baldy. You're 80 if you're a day!'

Some of the teachers at St Brats have really stupid names. Like our PE teacher. He's called Dicky Kneebone. Here are some of the others:

★ Our Chinese choir master, I Sing Sharp.
★ The maths mistress, Miss U D Vide, and Carrie Four, her assistant.
★ The teacher in charge of discipline, Ben Dover.
★ The mad zoology professor, Dr I M Barking.
★ Our animal-loving biology teacher, Ivor St Oat.

Of course it's not just teachers who have silly names. Our smelly and very dishonest headgirl is called Liza Lott. And the school bully, Ed Case, has a horrible girlfriend. She's called Bloody Mary.

THE SCHOOL BULLY

Jemima: What do you call an elderly needlework teacher whose name you can't remember?
William: Old sew and sew.

William: Why can't needlework teachers string two sentences together?
Jemima: Because they keep losing their thread.

William: My French teacher's really soppy.
Jemima: How do you know?
William: She put kisses next to all the answers on my exam paper.

Jemima: What do you call someone who teaches sums and wheezes at the same time?
William: A mathsmatic.

Jemima: The lady who takes us for English composition was standing outside school for ages and ages today.
William: She was probably waiting for Mr Write to come along.

Jemima: What do you call a geometry teacher who goes fishing at weekends?
William: A right angler.

PUNISHMENTS

DETENTION CLASS

Because Teach isn't allowed to hit us any more, he has to be extra, extra cunning when doshing out punishments that will make us beg for mercy. Us Brats have suffered everything in the following list – and we didn't cry once.

The Ten Worst Punishments in the World in Order of Absolute Yukky Horribleness

1) Eating cold macaroni cheese.

2) Eating two helpings of cold macaroni cheese.

3) Eating two helpings of very cold macaroni cheese standing in a bucket of school stew.

4) Eating three helpings of extremely cold macaroni cheese standing in a bucket of even colder stew during double chemistry.

A COMPUTER
CAN BE HANDY
FOR DOING LINES...

5) Eating four helpings of very, very cold macaroni cheese in a basin of much colder school stew during triple chemistry with a slimy toad in your underpants.

6) Eating five helpings of exceedingly chilly macaroni cheese standing in a bathful of glacial stew in quadruple chemistry with two slimy toads who hate each other fighting in your underpants while an earwig builds a nest in your armpit.

7) Eating six helpings of macaroni cheese that's so cold it's gone blue standing in a barrel of totally frozen stew in double quadruple chemistry with two families of slimy toads who loathe each other's guts playing hockey in your underpants while 20 earwigs build a skyscraper in

your armpit and you write out 100 times 'My PE teacher is very intelligent'.

8) Eating seven helpings of macaroni cheese that's so cold and lumpy you need an ice-breaker to mash it up standing in a swimming pool of rotting and frozen school stew in double treble quadruple chemistry with two warring tribes of slimy toads staging the toads' equivalent of the Olympic Games in your underpants, a colony of earwigs building a medium-sized new town in your armpit, you writing out 500 times 'My PE teacher is the most intelligent person I've ever met' and the school lavatory attendant deciding to use you as a brush.

9) Eating eight helpings of macaroni cheese that's so cold and lumpy it reminds you of frozen sick standing in a lake of completely rotting and totally yukky frozen stew in double double treble quadruple chemistry AND Latin

...IF YOU HAVEN'T GOT A COMPUTER GET AN OCTOPUS TO DO THEM

with a nation of slimy toads re-enacting the Second World War in your underpants while millions of earwigs build a new country in your armpit, you write out 500,000 times 'My PE teacher is the most intelligent person I've met since next door bought a gerbil', the school lavatory attendant uses you as a brush and you watch your worst enemy move into your bedroom at home and throw out all your favourite red Lego bricks.

10) Double PE.

For Most pupils, detention sessions last on average one hour...

... for others, however, it may last slightly longer.

Jemima: What goes klahc klahc ouch!? William: Chalk being thrown at you backwards over the teacher's shoulder.

CHAPTER 9

EXAMS/TESTS/REPORTS

The Brat Foolproof Exam Revision Technique

This method is guaranteed completely foolproof – follow it to the letter and prove you're a complete fool!!!

★ Do absolutely no revision.
★ Listen to the Wee Papa Girl Rappers all day instead.
★ Stay up late watching violent TV programmes (*Top of the Pops*, *John Craven's Newsround*, etc.) and develop big dark rings under your eyes.
★ Develop crush on Kylie Minogue or Wet Wet Wet.
★ Ignore parents when they say: 'You'll fail your exams if you don't pull your finger out.'
★ Fail to understand what you are supposed to pull your finger out of.
★ Sit exams.
★ Fail them.

IF YOU WANT TO CHEAT IN YOUR MATHS TEST, SMUGGLE IN A COMPUTER...

5×7=35
6×7=42...

... OR TEACH YOUR PARROT HIS MULTIPLICATION TABLES AND SNEAK HIM IN WITH YOU

How to pass all your exams with flying colours
1) Work extremely hard and have a very miserable life.
2) That's all.

Of course, if you're a real brat and you take our advice, your end-of-term report will be grottier than a stoat's laundry basket. If that's the case, fill in your name and give this to your parents instead.

NAME:

ENGLISH: A. Your child is the most brilliant I've ever taught. His/her essays read like vintage Dickens, and his/her poetry makes Shakespeare sound like an ill-educated football yob.

FRENCH: A+. Formidable! I have written to the Queen recommending your child for the post of ambassador to France with immediate effect.

GEOGRAPHY: A Never in the history of the world has anyone displayed such a grasp of geography. Your child is the first I have taught who knew what the capital of Burkino Faso was. In fact, your child is the first to have heard of Burkino Faso full stop. In fact I hadn't even heard of it until your child mentioned it....

HISTORY: A+. We are rewriting our history books to include the vital role your child made over half term at the peace summit between the United States and the Soviet Union. A fantastic contribution to world history, if I may so humbly suggest.

SCIENCE: I cannot think of a pupil who better deserves his/her Nobel Prize. Excellent.

SPORT: Obviously, so many talent scouts at the school grounds has created jealousy among less able pupils. But we would like to congratulate your child and wish him/her every success in the coming season playing for England.

① GIVE IT TO YOUR PARENTS TO READ — AND RISK SERIOUS INJURY

② EAT IT — BUT MAKE SURE YOU CHEW IT PROPERLY OR IT MAY GET STUCK IN YOUR THROAT.

③ MAKE IT INTO A TRENDY HAT.

④ USE IT AS A HANDKERCHIEF — WHO WANTS TO READ A REPORT THAT'S COVERED IN BOGIES?

⑤ ROLL IT UP AND USE AS A PEA SHOOTER

⑥ STICK A LOAD OF REPORTS TOGETHER AND USE AS A TOILET ROLL — THE PAPER'S A BIT SCRATCHY BUT IT'S A SURE WAY OF PUTTING YOUR PARENTS OFF OF READING THEM.

If the REAL report arrives at home and your parents pounce on it before you do, don't get depressed. Teachers always write rubbish, so use this special guide to translate it.

How to read your school report

EXCELLENT: You are a complete creep who spends weekends washing every piece of gravel on the headmistress's driveway BY HAND. You probably do your French teacher's ironing, too.

VERY, VERY ABLE: There is only one thing in the world that's better at sucking up than you – A VACUUM CLEANER.

AVERAGE/GOOD: BORING! Bet you wash your hands before meals, always say your prayers, comb your hair and do your homework without cheating. When you grow up, you will be either a traffic warden or the person who collects the fines on library books.

BELOW AVERAGE: Better. Most boys and girl are below average in lessons. They are more interested in the important things in life – such as catapults, breeding slugs in their duffle coat pockets and putting live stoats up the jumper of the school swot.

POOR: Well done. You worked hard this term at learning absolutely nothing and really enjoyed the time spent not learning it. Next term you must try harder to do even worse.

VERY, VERY POOR: Excellent. You really know how to make the most of your time in school. Your lying, cheating, stealing, fighting, bullying and rudeness were much improved and you have a promising future ahead of you. Or you might consider staying on at school, failing your exams and becoming a PE teacher.

It is highly recommended that you study extra-hard for chemistry exams...

... a great deal of satisfaction can be gained from your results.

RED POSE

Jemima: How can I be top in all my exams, William?
William: Stand on your desk when they read out the results, stupid.

HOLIDAYS/FREE-TIME

Holidays mean two things: no school and food poisoning. We Brats have been everywhere, so we know where it's good and where it's rubbish (i.e. where the teachers go).

Read this guide and tell your Mum and Dad where you want to catch food poisoning next year.

BLACKPOOL (ENGLAND)

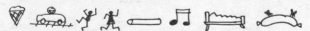

Full of yobs, slobs, fat people, noise, aggro, ice-cream, crowds, rowdiness and people being ill after eating too many greasy chips and too much candy floss. Teachers avoid it like the plague coz they're too stuck up. Highly recommended.

BENIDORM (SPAIN)

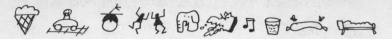

Just like Blackpool, only much hotter and sweatier with more poisonous junk food and undrinkable water. If you bump into swotty types or teachers 'brushing up' their Spanish, don't forget to introduce them to the local food. Brill!!!

LOIRE VALLEY (FRANCE)

Beautiful, picturesque part of France about a hundred miles from Paris with excellent food, friendly locals, low prices and lots of sunshine. Full of teachers in clapped out cars with camping equipment tied to the roof-racks. Avoid at all costs.

DISNEYWORLD (USA)

Brill, if you like standing in line for six hours to go on a thirty-second funfair ride. Take itching powder to reduce the length of the queue.

THE ANTARCTIC (ANTARCTICA)

Freezing cold, boring, cold, dull, icy, tedious and cold. BUT – very few teachers go there, so it's highly recommended.

KEY:

🍦 Ice-cream

🍎 Teachers

🍎 Teachers with stupid puppy dogs

📠 Yuppies

📠 Yuppies with puppies

🏃 Nightlife

🐘 Wildlife

Wild night life

👶 Babies

Rabies

Babies with rabies

🎢 Fun rides

Cartoon characters

🐧 Penguins

Rock

🎵 Rock and roll

🥖 Bread roll [stale]

Undrinkable water

Inedible food

🛏 Uncomfortable beds

Fat tourists who sit on you if you are not careful

The end of the school year is always an enjoyable time for everyone ...

... Most spend the six weeks holiday relaxing with their feet up.

75

THE CARETAKER

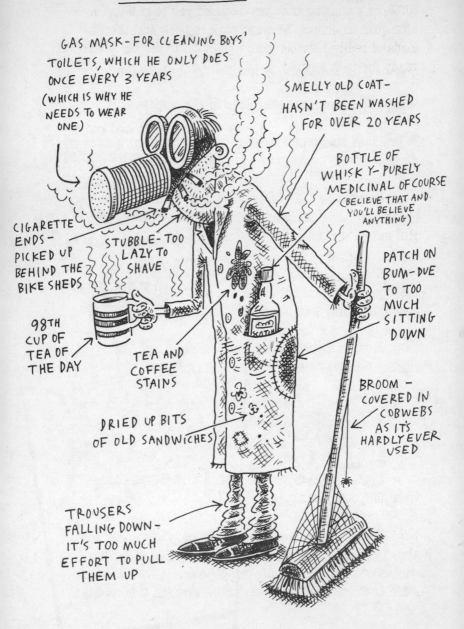

AND don't imagine that just because you're not there, all's quiet at school. We went back to peek and there's loads of really horrible things going on to get the place ready for next term.

What the school caretaker does in the holidays

★ Glues sharp new wooden splinters to chairs and desks ready to spear young fingers and legs.

★ Scrapes up old bits of chewing gum from under desks and sticks them into school clocks. (Makes clocks run slower so lessons drag on and on.)

★ With the School Cook, boils up cauldron of old Elastoplasts, dental braces, scabs and rotting cabbage leaves that will go into next term's stew.

★ Sprays changing rooms with Cheese and Onion Hockey Sock-flavoured perfume.

★ Greases the floor outside the staff room so teachers can yell at you: 'The corridors are NOT for sliding in. Skid once more and I'll put you in detention.'

★ Licks the teachers' cars clean and polishes them with his (only) hanky.

We Brats love to waste a lot of time on holiday. Nothing annoys grown-ups more than thinking we're enjoying ourselves but not doing anything 'constructive'. Here are some Brat-approved ways of getting through the holidays.

BEATING THE RUSH HOME
AT THE END OF TERM

Good ways to waste your free-time

★ COIN COLLECTING: Collecting other people's coins is technically theft, which is illegal if you get caught. Stick to stamps – get it?

★ RACKETS: Running a protection racket in your summer holidays like Al Capone is great fun and a really good way to get to know people in your area. Avoid the other kind of rackets – tennis and squash. These require a lot of running around, which can be tiring.

★ RAMBLING: This is an outdoor hobby for those who like to go on and on about things without really getting to the sort of ... um ... you know ... point. You don't need any equipment and you can ramble anywhere. Be warned : it can take all day – especially if you're good at it.

William: What do you call someone who catches measles at the start of term?
Jemima: Lucky.
William: What do you call it if someone catches measles at the start of the holidays?
Jemima: A very rash decision.

William: In the holidays, do you ever miss the teachers, Jemima?
Jemima: Only when my pea shooter jams.

Music teacher: William, I want you to use eyes, ears and brain for this interpretation, so watch me, breathe deeply, open up your lungs and put all your heart into it.
William: This is choir practice, you know, not an organ recital.

BED NOSE

CHAPTER

11

HOW TO HELP
COMIC RELIEF

There are lots of things you can do for Comic Relief. Most especially buy a red nose and organize some totally fab event to make millions of pounds of cash.

Now we've got lots of ideas of totally brill things we're going to be doing. But we're not going to tell you because we want to win the Radio One Golden Nose Awards for being Best Red Nose Supporters of All.

But to give you a bit of a hand, so you can come second, here is...

THE WILLIAM AND JEMIMA BRAT GUIDE TO TEN SCHOOLS WHO WERE BRILLIANT LAST YEAR

School: Our Lady Star of the Sea Primary School, Seaforth, Liverpool

Red Nose Romp: They had bingo, raffles and talent contests and Mrs Cooper dressed as an elf, Mrs Hogan as a fairy, and Mrs Rice as a vampire. (Crazy Girls!!!)

School: St Catherine's RC School, Moss Lane, Leyland
Red Nose Romp: They raised £125.12 by having a sponsored joke-telling to see how many jokes they could tell in 30 minutes. They told 157 jokes.

School: Caldecott Senior School, Abingdon, Oxon
Red Nose Romp: Pupils paid 10p each for the privilege of wearing their clothes backwards to school – and later they told stories about the most embarrassing things that had happened to them.

School: Strandtown Primary School, Belfast
Red Nose Romp: They wore red noses and they held a very successful sponsored Wellington Boot Throw. (Pong!!)

School: Blackdown County First and Middle School, Camberley, Surrey
Red Nose Romp: Pupils paid 20p not to wear school uniform and raised £86 by selling cakes, telling jokes in assembly and paying to wear fancy dress as well.

School: Mile End School, Aberdeen
Red Nose Romp: The whole school took part in a fancy-dress competition won by Matthew Maloney, dressed as a punk. A gel named Morag put on a lot of lipstick and kissed Scott for a sponsored kiss. She raised 65p. Susan kissed Christopher 10 times and raised 60p. With all the kissing, cakes and candy stalls, they raised £404.50.

School: Woolsey School, Devon
Red Nose Romp: Played pass-the-parcel backwards (*How do you do that?*) and musical bumps, where they stood up when the music stopped. And the teachers wore silly clothes to keep them company.

School: Ton Pentre Infant School, Mid-Glamorgan, Wales
Red Nose Romp: Their six-year-olds (starting young!!) took part in a sponsored colouring. They all had their faces painted as clowns and then were sponsored for every spot they had coloured in on their clown jackets.
(*Cunning ruse – imagine spots coming in useful at last!!!*)

School: St Chrysostom's CE. Primary School, Chorlton-on-Medlock, Manchester
Red Nose Romp: Class 8 put on a show to entertain the school – including a magician, ventriloquist, drums, 'Can't Can't Girls', rock singer, impressionist and a steel band. (*Jolly talented bunch!!*) They also wore fancy dress to school and did a sponsored swim in pyjamas and nightdresses and raised £279.30.

School: St Paul's School, Penrose St, London SE17
Red Nose Romp: Raised £415 by doing a sponsored hokey-cokey. They did 40 hokey-cokeys in 30 minutes – as well as wearing clown suits and painting their noses red.
(*That's hokey-cokey-okay by us!!!*)

School: Lea Primary School, Moorland Road, Harpenden
Red Nose Romp: Dared the Headmaster, Mr Boxer, to do a sponsored shop in Sainsbury's, wearing fancy dress!! Good on him!

And Mark Ollard of Carshalton Beeches raised £25 with his dog Suki who did a sponsored going-to-the-toilet-on-her-daily-walk. She went 47 times!!!!! (Well done, Suki-baby!!!)

Thanks to the following people for the info and help: Joseph Johnson, Aidan Walsh, Craig Bishop, Jennifer Hughes, Kirstie Lane, Richard French, Helen and Fiona in Aberdeen and Class 3 in Penrose Street.

If you do things like this, and raise the most money, you may become famous and appear in our book next year. Because some kids *do* become famous – while the rest become parents. And if your school's not doing anything, then try to do something on your own!!! Remember – every little penny helps. Last year, **every single 50p we got was enough to pay for injections to make sure a kid in Ethiopia or Sudan didn't die of six killer diseases.**

All donations should be addressed to:

```
           Comic Relief '89
           Peat Marwick McLintock
           P.O. Box 878
           London
           EC4Y 8AF
```

And Finally...

We wrote to some of the grown-up kids who are friends of Comic Relief, as a special little end-of-book treat for us all, and asked them to tell – **WITH ABSOLUTELY NO FIBBING** – about their lives at school, all those hundreds of years ago.

P.T.O. →

Here are some of the replies — we've left out all the soppy introductory letters, all the 'Dear William and Jemima, how fab to hear from you two, our favourite fans in the whole world' stuff, and just got down to the hardcore info...

CELEBRITIES' SCHOOL REPORT CARDS

NAME: Atkinson, Rowan
FAMOUS FOR: 'Not being of our world'
NICKNAME: Zoonie, Moonman, Green Man, then Monster
FIRST CRUSH: On a miniature tractor I saw at the Royal Show
MOST HATED SUBJECT: History
DID YOU EVER CHEAT: Yes
MOST HATED SCHOOL DINNER: Bread and butter pudding. I brought it up immediately
WHAT DO YOU MOST REGRET YOU DIDN'T DO: I nearly helped build a home-made bomb to blow up the cricket pavilion, but we all chickened out and blew a hole in a cliff instead
BEST REMEMBERED TEACHER: Mr Lamping, the Housemaster. No rational reason — we used to try to teach his two-year-old son to say rude words
SCHOOLDAYS WERE: The naughtiest of my life

NAME: Bremner, Rory
TYPE OF PUPIL: Swot and sports fanatic
FAMOUS FOR: Telling one joke too many
NICKNAME: Bill, Jock
MOST HATED SUBJECT: Maths, physics
DID YOU EVER CHEAT: Of course not er, yes, once or twice when I was in trouble
MOST HATED SCHOOL DINNER: Bread and butter pudding
WHAT DO YOU MOST REGRET YOU DID: Tackling one of my own team in front of an open goal and then shooting wide
WHAT DO YOU MOST REGRET YOU DIDN'T DO: Find a cure for acne
BEST REMEMBERED TEACHER: Derek Swift — my first public impersonation

NAME: Bruno, Frank
TYPE OF PUPIL: Sports fanatic
FAMOUS FOR: Studying
NICKNAME: Blackwall Tunnel
FIRST CRUSH: Grapes
MOST HATED SUBJECT: Teachers
DID YOU EVER CHEAT: Yes
MOST HATED SCHOOL DINNER: I loved all the food
WHAT DO YOU MOST REGRET YOU DID: Leave school
WHAT DO YOU MOST REGRET YOU DIDN'T DO: Start school
BEST REMEMBERED TEACHER: Sports teacher – good sparring partner
SCHOOLDAYS WERE: The hungriest of my life

NAME: Crane, Andy
TYPE OF PUPIL: Nearly the thinnest boy in the school
FAMOUS FOR: Being taught by my Dad
NICKNAME: Craney – how boring!
FIRST CRUSH: Debbie in primary school
MOST HATED SUBJECT: FRENCH!!!!! YEOK!!!!
DID YOU EVER CHEAT: Yes – especially in French homework
MOST HATED SCHOOL DINNER: Semolina with jam in the middle. I stuffed as much of it as I could in my cheeks and spat it down the loo
WHAT DO YOU MOST REGRET YOU DID: Swallowing some semolina
WHAT DO YOU MOST REGRET YOU DIDN'T DO: Feed the semolina to the dinner ladies
BEST REMEMBERED TEACHER: My Dad 'cause he was – My Dad!
SCHOOLDAYS WERE: The tiredest of my life

RUT NOSE

NAME: Craven, John
TYPE OF PUPIL: Total weed and the thinnest boy in school
FAMOUS FOR: Being caned for snowballing the girls
NICKNAME: Craven 'A' – after the cigarettes
FIRST CRUSH: Sandra Ibbotson (but her daughter says will I please not mention her name again!)
MOST HATED SUBJECT: Physics
MOST HATED SCHOOL DINNER: Tough, stringy meat and soggy cabbage. Got to be head of table so served it to everyone else!
WHAT DO YOU MOST REGRET YOU DID: Learn the euphonium
WHAT DO YOU MOST REGRET YOU DIDN'T DO: Homework
BEST REMEMBERED TEACHER: Mr White, the chemistry teacher. He'd write out a complicated theory then say: 'Watch the blackboard while I go through it!'
SCHOOLDAYS WERE: The average-est of my life

NAME: Curry, Mark
TYPE OF PUPIL: Total weed but precocious
NICKNAME: Vindaloo
FIRST CRUSH: Emma Peel in *The Avengers*
MOST HATED SUBJECT: Maths, maths and maths
DID YOU EVER CHEAT: Yes
MOST HATED SCHOOL DINNER: Spam fritters followed by semolina. One day, the horrendous task of having to face spam fritters was cut short by a girl being sick all over the table and my dinner (probably improving the flavour)
WHAT DO YOU MOST REGRET YOU DID: Never coming in the first 30 in cross-country running
WHAT DO YOU MOST REGRET YOU DIDN'T DO: I never did anything naughty in the bike shed – I just put my bike in there
BEST REMEMBERED TEACHER: The social studies teacher who looked like Sooty
SCHOOLDAYS WERE: The worst, boringest and scariest of my life

FED NOSE

NAME: Daniels, Paul
TYPE OF PUPIL: Total weed who thought he was a precociously cool sex bomb
FAMOUS FOR: Pouring rice pudding into geography teacher's lap
NICKNAME: Shadrach
FIRST CRUSH: Irene Hewitt
MOST HATED SUBJECT: Latin
DID YOU EVER CHEAT: No – too scared
MOST HATED SCHOOL DINNER: Fatty meat stew – I left it
WHAT DO YOU MOST REGRET YOU DIDN'T DO: Understand that most of the stuff I learnt I'd never use
SCHOOLDAYS WERE: The scariest of my life

NAME: Davidson, Jim
TYPE OF PUPIL: Bit of a sports fanatic with very thin legs
FAMOUS FOR: Messing about and doing impressions of teachers
NICKNAME: Jock
FIRST CRUSH: Susan Sergeant (now married and lives in Northampton)
MOST HATED SUBJECT: Religion
DID YOU EVER CHEAT: Yes
MOST HATED SCHOOL DINNER: Butter beans – I shovelled them into a hole in the ventilation
WHAT DO YOU MOST REGRET YOU DID: Got slung out
WHAT DO YOU MOST REGRET YOU DIDN'T DO: Learn anything
BEST REMEMBERED TEACHER: Mr Davis the woodwork teacher – he could chat through three periods so we did no woodwork
SCHOOLDAYS WERE: The start of my life!

BLED NOSE

NAME: Edwards, Eddie 'the Eagle'
TYPE OF PUPIL: Sports fanatic
NICKNAME: 'VG'
FIRST CRUSH: Geraldine and Joanne Modford
MOST HATED SUBJECT: Science
MOST HATED SCHOOL DINNER: Semolina – I stuck it in my blazer pocket
WHAT DO YOU MOST REGRET YOU DID: Hitting someone who wore glasses
WHAT DO YOU MOST REGRET YOU DIDN'T DO: Kiss Julie Harvie on first date
BEST REMEMBERED TEACHER: Mickie Miller, the sports teacher who introduced me to skiing
SCHOOLDAYS WERE: The naughtiest, boringest, scariest and hungriest of my life

NAME: Fox, Samantha
TYPE OF PUPIL: Precociously cool sex kitten
NICKNAME: Foxy
FIRST CRUSH: David Cassidy
MOST HATED SUBJECT: Maths
DID YOU EVER CHEAT: Yes
MOST HATED SCHOOL DINNER: Carrots and sprouts. I'd smile at a boy and get him to eat them for me
WHAT DO YOU MOST REGRET YOU DID: Flicking ink on the nuns' habits
WHAT DO YOU MOST REGRET YOU DIDN'T DO: Owning up to the above
BEST REMEMBERED TEACHER: Sister Inkspot – well, that's what we called her
SCHOOLDAYS WERE: The naughtiest of my life

NAME: Greene, Sarah
TYPE OF PUPIL: Bully, swot, total weed, total zero nobody knew existed, precociously cool sex kitten, sports fanatic, teacher's pet, fattest, thinnest and ugliest girl in the school plus a naughty little ring-leader. Phew!
FAMOUS FOR: Causing trouble and letting others take the rap
NICKNAME: Greeno, you naughty rascal!
FIRST CRUSH: School treacle pudding and custard
MOST HATED SUBJECT: Anything involving running about in the cold and having to score goals
MOST HATED SCHOOL DINNER: Spam fritters and cabbage. I once threw it up on the back of the 24 bus. After that I hid the spam fritters in my skirt pocket and chucked them away in the playground
WHAT DO YOU MOST REGRET YOU DID: Shooting a Biro spring up my English teacher's nose
WHAT DO YOU MOST REGRET YOU DIDN'T DO: Take the spring out
BEST REMEMBERED TEACHER: The one with the Biro spring sticking out of her nose

NAME: Large, Eddie
TYPE OF PUPIL: Sports fanatic
NICKNAME: Macca – my real name is McGinnis
FIRST CRUSH: Jane in the *Daily Mirror*
MOST HATED SUBJECT: Science
MOST HATED SCHOOL DINNER: I ate everything
WHAT DO YOU MOST REGRET YOU DID: Something disgusting in the science teacher's wastepaper bin
WHAT DO YOU MOST REGRET YOU DIDN'T DO: Punching the science teacher on the gob
BEST REMEMBERED TEACHER: Miss Morton because of netball practice
SCHOOLDAYS WERE: The daftest of my life

NAME: McCoy, Sylvester
TYPE OF PUPIL: Total weed
FAMOUS FOR: Picking his nose
NICKNAME: Smithy
FIRST CRUSH: Elspeth Calder
MOST HATED SUBJECT: Military exercises. I was kicked out of the schoolboy army and made to do art instead
DID YOU EVER CHEAT: Yes. That's what school is all about
MOST HATED SCHOOL DINNER: Mushy peas – I put them in my welly boots
WHAT DO YOU MOST REGRET YOU DID: Getting up one day, going to school and discovering it was Saturday

NAME: McGough, Roger
FAMOUS FOR: Talent. Rhyming. Urbanity. Truth. Humour
NICKNAME: The T.R.U.T.H. (which stands for Talent, Rhyming, Urbanity, Truth, Humour)
FIRST CRUSH: Joan Taylor
MOST HATED SUBJECT: Shipbuilding
DID YOU EVER CHEAT: No – I got others to do it for me
MOST HATED SCHOOL DINNER: Corned Beef Ash. There were two cigarette stumps in it – honest!
WHAT DO YOU MOST REGRET YOU DID: Tell Mr O'Hanlon that chemistry was a waste of time
WHAT DO YOU MOST REGRET YOU DIDN'T DO: Tell Joan Taylor what I've just told three million people now
BEST REMEMBERED TEACHER: Mr O'Hanlon, because he grabbed me by the left ear, pushed my right hand behind my back, picked up a bunsen burner...

NAME: Mole, Adrian
TYPE OF PUPIL: I do not fit into any normal category
FAMOUS FOR: My literary precocity. I was, indeed I still am, an expert on the books of Nevil Shute
NICKNAME: Joe Ninety, after a TV puppet who wore glasses, and Brains
FIRST CRUSH: After Nevil Shute I fell in love with a marmalade-haired minx called Pandora Braithewaite
MOST HATED SUBJECT: Swimming. I hated the display of unhealthy naked flesh, especially my own
MOST HATED SCHOOL DINNER: Oxtail stew on Mondays. I secreted the little round bones about my person and took them home to the dog who is not known for its discriminatory eating habits
WHAT DO YOU MOST REGRET YOU DID: Not paying attention in sex lessons
WHAT DO YOU MOST REGRET YOU DIDN'T DO: I wish I had taken O level drama. The world, I fear, has lost a fine actor in me
SCHOOLDAYS WERE: The surrealist of my life

NAME: Planer, Nigel (Piggo)
TYPE OF PUPIL: Bully – and no, I don't regret it
NICKNAME: Tantrum or Piggo
MOST HATED SCHOOL DINNER: Rice pudding. I would ask for a 'small' and swill it round the plate like a leftover 'big'.
BEST REMEMBERED TEACHER: John Leonard ('Lenny') who read to us but never finished a book so we wanted to read just to finish something

SHED
NOSE

NAME: Potter, Simon
TYPE OF PUPIL: Sports fanatic who wanted to be a precociously cool sex bomb
FAMOUS FOR: Distributing 'fart' devices in the second year. A fart device was a piece of coat hanger bent into a horseshoe with an elastic band stretched across. A washer was attached to the elastic band. All you had to do was wind up the band and reverberate the washer against a text book for full effect
NICKNAME: Muff, Trixie and Pottsy
FIRST CRUSH: Pauline Dunn
MOST HATED SUBJECT: Maths
DID YOU EVER CHEAT: Yes
MOST HATED SCHOOL DINNER: Fish in rock hard batter, tinned tomatoes and lumpy mashed potato. I made Wayne Fleet eat it. He was asthmatic and considerably weaker than me
WHAT DO YOU MOST REGRET YOU DID: Sitting next to Wayne Fleet after a meal like that
WHAT DO YOU MOST REGRET YOU DIDN'T DO: Get more bold with Kathryn Lowrey
BEST REMEMBERED TEACHER: Mr Jones – a maths teacher with buffalo breath. Vindictive, petty-minded and enough to make me ashamed of being Welsh. Except I'm not!

NAME: Rice, Anneka
TYPE OF PUPIL: Swot, sports fanatic and teacher's pet
NICKNAME: Uncle Ben (get it?)
FIRST CRUSH: Mr Judd, my trampoline teacher
MOST HATED SUBJECT: Latin
DID YOU EVER CHEAT: Only at Latin
MOST HATED SCHOOL DINNER: Liver – I hid it in my pencil case (I got through a lot of pencil-cases)
WHAT DO YOU MOST REGRET YOU DID: Latin
WHAT DO YOU MOST REGRET YOU DIDN'T DO: Punch Wendy M— on the nose
BEST REMEMBERED TEACHER: Mr Judd (see above)
SCHOOLDAYS WERE: The best-forgotten-est of my life

ROAD NOSE

NAME: Robinson, Tony

TYPE OF PUPIL: Total weed and the smallest boy in the school. I'd love to be a bully but I'm too scared

FAMOUS FOR: Being such a total git (like Baldrick, actually)

NICKNAME: Mighty Mouse

FIRST CRUSH: Muffin the Mule (and it still is)

MOST HATED SUBJECT: Maths

DID YOU EVER CHEAT: Yes, but it didn't do any good. I cheated in my O levels and still only got four

MOST HATED SCHOOL DINNER: School greens. I put them in my pockets and cleaned them out at the end of the week

WHAT DO YOU MOST REGRET YOU DID: Wear short trousers in the sixth form

WHAT DO YOU MOST REGRET YOU DIDN'T DO: Ask out Anne Woodruff

BEST REMEMBERED TEACHER: Our PT teacher was called Ron Pickering and he became a famous TV sports commentator but I remember when he used to hit my bottom with a plimsoll because my hair was too long

SCHOOLDAYS WERE: Easily the worst of my life

NAME: Ross, Jonathan

TYPE OF PUPIL: Total weed and thinnest boy in the school

FAMOUS FOR: Drawing rude pictures of the teachers

NICKNAME: Rossy (boring, I know, occasionally spiced up to Ross-the-Toss)

FIRST CRUSH: Maxine Stevens, aged 5, though Kay Gillingham came close!

MOST HATED SUBJECT: PE

DID YOU EVER CHEAT: Yes

MOST HATED SCHOOL DINNER: I hated school dinners full stop. I would mash it up small in the corner of the plate and hope the dinner lady thought I had eaten it. Never worked.

WHAT DO YOU MOST REGRET YOU DID: Dropped a big stone on my friend Jimmy's head

WHAT DO YOU MOST REGRET YOU DIDN'T DO: Punch the school bully

BEST REMEMBERED TEACHER: Mrs Bendall because she gave me Spangles

SCHOOLDAYS WERE: The scruffiest of my life

NAME: Schofield, Phillip
TYPE OF PUPIL: A total weed who dreamed of being a precociously cool sex bomb
FAMOUS FOR: Being a naught joker in the classes I hated and a swot in those I liked
NICKNAME: Flipper
FIRST CRUSH: Susan Roberts and my bike
MOST HATED SUBJECT: Maths
DID YOU EVER CHEAT: Once or twice or three or four ... or five times
MOST HATED SCHOOL DINNER: Semolina – I offered it to the school fattie who ate anything
WHAT DO YOU MOST REGRET YOU DID: Take private maths lessons because they didn't work. I could have been out on my bike
WHAT DO YOU MOST REGRET YOU DIDN'T DO: Learn a musical instrument
BEST REMEMBERED TEACHER: Mrs Grace,the art teacher. She could have laughed – but didn't
SCHOOLDAYS WERE: The naughtiest of my life

NAME: Smith, Mel
TYPE OF PUPIL: Swot and sports fanatic and the ugliest *girl* in the school
FAMOUS FOR: Being in the school play and captain of the school rugby team at the same time – phew, what a guy!
NICKNAME: Smith! (The ! was very important)
FIRST CRUSH: Miss Double, my primary school headmistress
MOST HATED SUBJECT: Geography
MOST HATED SCHOOL DINNER: Liver in that thin gravy with tiny lumps in it. Otherwise I ate *anything*
WHAT DO YOU MOST REGRET YOU DID: Telling everyone I liked physics
WHAT DO YOU MOST REGRET YOU DIDN'T DO: Telling everyone I hated physics and wanted to read chemistry, maths and brass rubbing at A level
BEST REMEMBERED TEACHER: Mr 'Chunky' Constable – a real idiot as I remember (he taught physics)
SCHOOLDAYS WERE: The best and scariest of my life

NAME: Smith (Smif), Mike
TYPE OF PUPIL: Swot until the age of 11, then a total weed
FAMOUS FOR: Sticking out ears and a 'pregnant' stomach
NICKNAME: Big Ears, Preggers
FIRST CRUSH: The French assistant and the biology teacher
DID YOU EVER CHEAT: Yes
MOST HATED SCHOOL DINNER: I hated all of it. I was the only
one who fought to go to the *back* of the queue
WHAT DO YOU MOST REGRET YOU DID: Balancing a wastepaper
bin over a door before Mr Fife (maths) arrived
WHAT DO YOU MOST REGRET YOU DIDN'T DO: Visit him in
hospital
BEST REMEMBERED TEACHER: Er, you guessed!
SCHOOLDAYS WERE: The longest of my life

NAME: Wogan, Terry
TYPE OF PUPIL: Precociously cool sex bomb, sports fanatic,
teacher's pet and the fattest boy in the school
FAMOUS FOR: An oily charm
NICKNAME: Rut Gonad
FIRST CRUSH: Sister Agnes
MOST HATED SUBJECT: Sums
DID YOU EVER CHEAT: Never – I'm a Catholic
MOST HATED SCHOOL DINNER: My mother's sandwiches
BEST REMEMBERED TEACHER: Sister Agnes and Sister Mary
Frances
SCHOOLDAYS WERE: The worst of my life

ATTACK OF THE KILLER RED NOSES

NAME: Wilde, Kim (real name Smith)
TYPE OF PUPIL: Total zero nobody even knew existed
FAMOUS FOR: Reminding everyone when my birthday was by writing the date on the blackboard
NICKNAME: Smithy, of course
FIRST CRUSH: A little boy with golden hair called Armin
MOST HATED SUBJECT: Needlework, even though Nicky Faldo's mother taught me
DID YOU EVER CHEAT: Yes
MOST HATED SCHOOL DINNER: I was a real pig. I loved it all – everything
WHAT DO YOU MOST REGRET YOU DID: Worry so much about exams. What a waste they turned out to be
WHAT DO YOU MOST REGRET YOU DIDN'T DO: Get the lead in *Hiawatha*
BEST REMEMBERED TEACHER: The crazed science teacher who really scared me. He salivated like a rabid dog when he got angry and his eyes pierced through his spectacles
SCHOOLDAYS WERE: The naughtiest of my life